Choose Your Own Journey

Under the Sea

Written by
Susie Brooks

Kane Miller
A DIVISION OF EDC PUBLISHING

Illustrated by
Tracy Cottingham

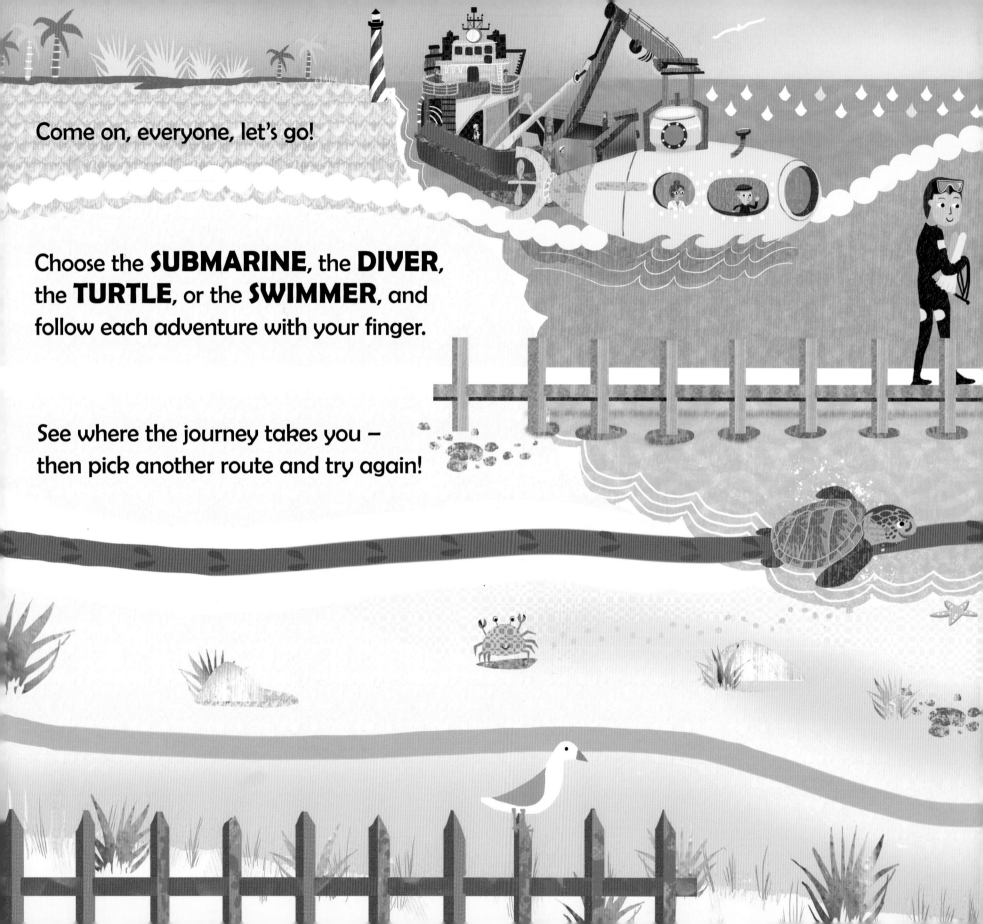

Come on, everyone, let's go!

Choose the **SUBMARINE**, the **DIVER**, the **TURTLE**, or the **SWIMMER**, and follow each adventure with your finger.

See where the journey takes you – then pick another route and try again!

It's a busy day on the bustling beach, but we're all **WHOOSHING** on the waves . . .

The diver's boat **ZOOMS** away, leaving the submarine and turtle **bobbing** behind!

It's time to dive in, swimmer . . .
kick your legs with a big **SPLASH!**

Water is whirling as windsurfers **WHIZZ**,
and riders squeal, "**WHEEEEEEE!**"

A surfer stands up on a giant **wave** and . . .
WHOOPS – look where you're going, turtle!

The diver's boat is in a hurry –
there's no time to stop and play.

A pod of dolphins join in the fun,
LEAPING, DIVING, and **WHISTLING**.

It's time to stop for a photo if you're in the submarine or boat.

Come on, swimmer, you can splash along with the dolphins.

Up ahead there's a sandy island, sparkling in the sunshine. Who wants a picnic?

Swimmer, we've got your favorite
ice cream . . . your journey ends right here.
SLURP!

GLUG, GLUG, GLUG, let's take a dive,
deep down under the ocean . . .

Say hello to the submarine, turtle!

Diver, where have you gone with your **flip-flapping flippers?**

Inside the yellow submarine, the scientists are excited.
There's so much to see on the colorful **coral reef** . . .

But **beware** of the hungry **SHARK**, turtle and diver!

Animals are **hiding** and **peeping**, scuttling and creeping, in and out of the rocks.

The submarine steers slowly past, playing peekaboo.

Can you see a big black-and-yellow fish, swimming with all the little ones?

Wait a minute – that's not a fish, it's the diver **racing** along!

CHIRP, CHIRP, CHIRP, FLIPPETY-FLAP . . . what's that commotion in the water?

It's a mass of traveling turtles!
The submarine slows down to watch.

Turtle, this is the end of your adventure.
Your friends have come to take you home.

BRRRRR, it's **dark** and **c-c-cold** down here in the deep water.

The submarine is searching for something, but it's not the big, smiley whale.

The diver pauses to rescue a crab
caught up in some plastic.

What's this? A spooky **SHIPWRECK**, with creatures lurking inside.

Under the light of the submarine,
the diver bravely takes a peek.

CREEEEAAK!

An octopus waves eight wings
as the submarine and diver

What's under the deck of this creaky wreck?

Now the only sounds are
a **RUMBLE, GURGLE, SWOOSH,**
chasing the submarine down a ravine.

Deeper and deeper . . .

Darker and darker . . .

Who will we find around
the next corner?

BOO! It's a **GIANT SQUID,**
with an eye bigger than your head . . .

Submarine, take a picture and make some notes.
Your mission is now complete!